The Women of Our Time® Series

DOROTHEA LANGE: *Life Through the Camera*
BABE DIDRIKSON: *Athlete of the Century*
ELEANOR ROOSEVELT: *First Lady of the World*
DIANA ROSS: *Star Supreme*
BETTY FRIEDAN: *A Voice for Women's Rights*
MARGARET THATCHER: *Britain's "Iron Lady"*
DOLLY PARTON: *Country Goin' to Town*
OUR GOLDA: *The Story of Golda Meir*
MARTINA NAVRATILOVA: *Tennis Power*
MOTHER TERESA: *Sister to the Poor*
WINNIE MANDELA: *The Soul of South Africa*
GRANDMA MOSES: *Painter of Rural America*
MARY McLEOD BETHUNE: *Voice of Black Hope*
LAURA INGALLS WILDER: *Growing Up in the Little House*
MARGARET MEAD: *The World Was Her Family*
CAROL BURNETT: *The Sound of Laughter*
RACHEL CARSON: *Pioneer of Ecology*
SHIRLEY TEMPLE BLACK: *Actress to Ambassador*
JULIE BROWN: *Racing Against the World*
JULIETTE GORDON LOW: *America's First Girl Scout*
BEVERLY SILLS: *America's Own Opera Star*
ASTRID LINDGREN: *Storyteller to the World*
HELEN KELLER: *A Light for the Blind*
HENRIETTA SZOLD: *Israel's Helping Hand*
AMELIA EARHART: *Courage in the Sky*
SANDRA DAY O'CONNOR: *Justice for All*

SANDRA DAY O'CONNOR

JUSTICE FOR ALL

BY BEVERLY GHERMAN
Illustrated by Robert Masheris

VIKING

For Deborah Brodie, who dared to take a chance on me

VIKING
Published by the Penguin Group
Viking Penguin, a division of Penguin Books USA Inc.,
375 Hudson Street, New York, New York 10014, U.S.A.
Penguin Books Ltd, 27 Wrights Lane, London W8 5TZ, England
Penguin Books Australia Ltd, Ringwood, Victoria, Australia
Penguin Books Canada Ltd, 2801 John Street, Markham, Ontario, Canada L3R 1B4
Penguin Books (N.Z.) Ltd, 182–190 Wairau Road, Auckland 10, New Zealand

Penguin Books Ltd, Registered Offices: Harmondsworth, Middlesex, England

First published in 1991 by Viking Penguin, a division of Penguin Books USA Inc.
1   3   5   7   9   10   8   6   4   2
Text copyright © Beverly Gherman, 1991
Illustrations copyright © Robert Masheris, 1991
All rights reserved

WOMEN OF OUR TIME® is a registered trademark of Viking Penguin, a division of
Penguin Books USA Inc.

Library of Congress Cataloging in Publication Data
Gherman, Beverly,
Sandra Day O'Connor / by Beverly Gherman ;
illustrated by Robert Masheris.
p.   cm.—(Women of our time)
Summary: A biography that follows Sandra Day O'Connor from her childhood on an
Arizona ranch, through her days as a young lawyer, to her appointment as the first
female to be named to the Supreme Court.
ISBN 0-670-82756-8
1. O'Connor, Sandra Day, 1930—Juvenile literature.
2. Judges—United States—Biography—Juvenile literature.
[1. O'Connor, Sandra Day, 1930–   2. Judges.   3. United States.
Supreme Court—Biography.]   I. Masheris, Robert, ill.   II. Title.   III. Series.
KF8745.O25G46   1991   347.73'2634—dc20
[B]   [347.3073534]   90-42033   CIP   AC   [B]

Printed in the United States of America
Set in Garamond #3

*Special thanks to Justice O'Connor and her friends, who shared their time
and memories with me*

CONTENTS

CHAPTER 1

Raging for Rain   3

CHAPTER 2

Leaving the Lazy B   11

CHAPTER 3

Down on the "Farm"   19

CHAPTER 4

Love and Law   27

CHAPTER 5

Tactful but Tough   34

CHAPTER 6

Supreme Court Justice   42

About This Book   57

SANDRA DAY O'CONNOR
JUSTICE FOR ALL

1

Raging for Rain

Sometimes when it didn't rain for weeks on end, the ground turned to dust and the juicy clumps of grass shrivelled and died. Sandra Day watched the cattle search for food. She studied the endless blue sky for any sign of clouds and kept asking the blazing sun, "Why can't it rain?"

Helping her father repair a broken fence, she noticed him looking at the sky. She knew what he was thinking. Without rain, the cattle on the Day family's Lazy B Ranch would go hungry and die.

Years later, Sandra remembered how she had

"raged inwardly because they didn't have rain—enough rain." She wanted to know "why God wouldn't want to make it rain and keep things going."

Just when they were ready to give up, storm clouds formed overhead. From inside their small adobe house, the family welcomed the rain. There would be enough moisture to soak through the earth. Soon the grasses would stir and sprout. The grazing cattle would have food.

Sandra knew they were out of danger this time. She couldn't wait to get outside into the sweet, clear air. Saddling her horse, Chico, she rode in search of

greasewood bushes. After the rain, they had "the most glorious smell in the world." That could help her forget how worried she had been.

She knew the area well. Even before she could walk, her father had swung her onto his horse. Her dark ringlets bobbed, her hazel eyes sparkled as she rode high above the ground, protected by her father's strong arms.

She soon learned to ride on her own horse. In time, she was able to help her father and the cowboys mend the fences and grease the windmill.

She learned to give the cattle shots against disease,

to brand the young calves during roundups, and to drive the truck or the tractor. Her father expected her to do those things and to do them well. After all, she was part of the team. It didn't matter that she was only seven, and a girl. Everyone on the ranch pitched in to do the work.

From her earliest years, Sandra assumed she would become a cattle rancher in Arizona just as her father and grandfather before her had been. She loved the family's Lazy B Ranch.

The ranch was set in a rugged corner of Arizona, a land of little rainfall. Sandra's grandfather, Henry Clay Day, had first driven a small herd of cattle from Mexico to Arizona in the 1880s, 30 years before Arizona became a state. The cattle he bought were already branded with a lazy letter B, lying down on the job. H. C. Day chose to name his ranch after the Lazy B brand. But he knew he couldn't be lazy if this first cattle ranch in the area would succeed.

When H. C. died, he left the ranch to his son, Harry Day, Sandra's father. Harry wanted to get a college education. He had his heart set on going to Stanford University, but that was no longer possible. He was needed to take over the ranch and keep it from failing.

Sandra's mother, Ada Mae Wilkey, had moved from a Duncan, Arizona, ranch to El Paso, Texas. It was a lively city, with a fine library and symphony hall. She attended good schools and travelled to Europe. Then she went on to graduate from the University of Arizona.

Once she met Harry Day, there was no one else for her. She and Harry were married in September of 1927.

Ada Mae "dearly loved" her new husband. She was not at all concerned about leaving city ways for life on a remote ranch. Hard work was not new to her. She and Harry were a handsome and determined pair, convinced they would succeed at ranching. They lived in a small adobe house, built brick upon brick from the red earth of Arizona.

In those early years, they had little money for extras, such as indoor plumbing, electricity, or a telephone. Yet they felt it was important to order magazines and buy books from a book club. They wanted to know what was happening in the outside world.

Harry studied every article he could find about solar heating. He became the first rancher in Greenlee County to install panels to heat the family's water. He also developed methods of flood control so useful that the other ranchers copied them. Gradually he improved the house with electricity and added a barn.

Just before Sandra was born, Ada Mae returned to her parents' home. There were no hospitals near the Lazy B. Sandra was born in an El Paso hospital on March 26, 1930.

Sandra spent her first five years on the Lazy B, learning about life on a vast desert where each evening's sunset was splashed against the sky. There were few people, and fewer trees. She learned to value the way people who worked on the ranch helped one another. She learned that hard work was expected and whining was not.

Because there were no nearby neighbors, Sandra became very attached to the ranch animals. She had a tame bobcat whose purring echoed through the small house. Pet goats lived nearby, a family of skunks nested under the porch, and raccoons visited often. She had been grooming and feeding her own horse all along.

Sandra was busy most of the time, helping her father or her mother with the chores. She might climb up the tall water tower behind her father, carefully taking

one rung at a time, hand over hand, one foot following the other. From the tower, they could see for miles around. And they could grease the windmill. That kept it working smoothly, pumping up groundwater which was stored in a large metal tank. It would never pump enough water to irrigate the dry earth, but it could be used for the cattle to drink when there was no rain.

For the Day family, there were constant reminders of the power nature held over their well-being. Weeks without rain could be followed by violent storms, lightning crashing across the sky in search of a tall boulder, a chimney, or an open window. Once Ada Mae had been working at the kitchen sink and moved away just as lightning crackled right on the spot where she had been standing.

Even when she was grown, Sandra remembered "the sense of helplessness" she felt living on a remote ranch. "There were times when it was very grim," she admitted. But the worries were never strong enough to make her stop wanting to become a cattle rancher.

2

Leaving the Lazy B

When Sandra was five years old, it was time for her to go to school. There were no schools near the ranch, but Ada Mae did not feel this was a problem. She had been a teacher and she would teach Sandra at home. At first, it worked out just fine. Soon, however, Ada Mae realized her daughter needed to be with other children.

Harry and Ada Mae did not want Sandra to travel long hours every morning to reach school and every evening to get home. The roads were terrible and the distances too great. They finally decided that Sandra should live with Grandmother Wilkey in El Paso and attend the Radford Girls' School. She would be able to come home to the ranch for all the holidays and school vacations.

Sandra was very excited about going to school and especially about taking the train to Grandmother Wilkey's. If she sat next to the window, Sandra could watch the hills fly past and the mountains rise and twist before her as the train crossed through New Mexico and then dipped south into Texas. Before she knew it, three hours had passed and they were pulling into the El Paso station, the engine loudly whistling its arrival. There was Grandmother Wilkey waving at her from the platform.

Sandra loved her young, lively grandmother. Sometimes she felt like she had two caring mothers. Grandmother Wilkey became her school mother. Ada Mae was her ranch mother.

Everyone at Radford School was friendly to Sandra. Still, she felt homesick for the ranch and her parents. To keep them close to her, Sandra taught her new Radford friends, Cita and Paquita, how to "play ranch." Each of them pretended to be a cattle rancher or a cowboy, riding on her horse to round up the wandering animals. They rode, slapping their sides, calling out to each other, and pretending they were on the Lazy B. Sandra soon felt a little less homesick.

She also brought her friends to visit the ranch whenever there was a school vacation. There were real horses to ride, real duties to perform, and lots to explore. In the evenings, no matter what the girls were doing, all the lights went out at 8:30. Harry's new generator provided only so much electrical power.

On one trip, Cita and Sandra got on the train together. Wearing their best outfits made them feel much more grown-up than their almost-eight years. Sandra, with her dark curly hair and bright hazel eyes, chose her brown-and-green plaid dress, white socks, and brown oxford shoes. Cita wore her red wool suit and let her blonde hair hang loose under a felt bowler hat.

Harry picked them up at the station and drove them back to the ranch in his jeep. On the way, he showed them the blossoming white flowers of the soapweed plant. He pointed out young calves sticking as close as possible to their mothers' sides.

As a special treat, Ada Mae took them into Lordsburg, New Mexico, to pick up the mail and magazines, including the latest *National Geographic* or *Saturday Evening Post.* They dropped off the family's dirty clothes to be washed and ironed by a laundress in town. Then the three of them stopped at the hotel for afternoon tea or a cool soda pop.

The visits were never long enough. One afternoon,

Sandra and Cita had all their belongings packed. They would be leaving for the station in a short time. Instead, they decided to sneak away and hide in the haystack out back. They hid themselves so well they weren't found in time to catch the train. Harry had to drive them to Separ, the stop after Lordsburg. But he didn't lose his temper. He knew Sandra felt "sad every time she had to leave home and go off to school."

It was even worse when she turned eight and her sister Ann was born. Sandra wanted to stay at the ranch to help with the baby. When her brother Alan was born two years later, leaving became harder than ever.

At school, Sandra still made believe she was on the ranch, but she also had to keep up with her schoolwork. By the fourth grade, she would have to give her three-minute extemporaneous (say "ek-stem-por-ANE-e-us") speech before the whole school. She would have to make up her ideas right on the spot. In her mind, Sandra kept practicing: "Dr. Templin, faculty, and fellow students . . ." That is how they were expected to begin their speeches.

Their headmistress, Dr. Templin, expected the girls to learn their formal subjects, as well as to use the best of manners at all times. Each student was invited to lunch with Dr. Templin at least once during the year to show her table manners. That was bad enough. But the extemporaneous speech worried them more.

When it was your turn, you picked a slip of paper listing the topic you were to discuss. You could take a few minutes to think. Then you were expected to stand in front of the whole student body and begin, "Dr. Templin, faculty, and fellow students . . ." It didn't matter how scared you felt, how wobbly or weak your voice sounded, or how wet your face and underarms became. You carried on. It prepared you for the future.

Dr. Templin collected autographed photographs of well-known people. She framed them and hung them along the halls. The girls would see them every day as they waited to enter the dining room. Some of the faces were very familiar, such as President Franklin Roosevelt and First Lady, Eleanor Roosevelt. The girls recognized movie stars like Shirley Temple, Jeanette MacDonald, Nelson Eddy, and Mickey Rooney. Ice skater Sonja Henie was a special favorite.

Other faces were not as familiar, but Dr. Templin wanted the girls to learn the names and faces of the musicians, writers, and scientists of the 1930s. If the girls touched the framed photographs, they had to clean off the fingerprints and smears they caused.

In 1941, when the United States entered World War II, its enemies—Germany, Italy, and Japan—

seemed very far away from the Lazy B. Yet men were being drafted to fight in the war. Sandra's parents read the daily war news in the paper and followed events in their magazines. They listened to their radio whenever they could get it to work.

At Radford School, the students were also keeping up with events. They were learning about the countries in Europe and Asia that were at war.

Sandra continued to live with Grandmother Wilkey and attend Radford School through the seventh grade. Then she insisted on returning to the ranch for the eighth grade. Her brother and sister were growing up and she wanted to be part of the family. She planned to get up every morning before sunrise. Then her parents could drop her off at a nearby ranch. There she and another student would meet the school bus that would take them to Lordsburg.

Sandra refused to think of the distance or the terrible condition of the roads or the fact that she would not get back to the Lazy B until after sunset every evening. She would at least have time with Ann and Alan on the weekends.

She managed to keep up that difficult schedule for the whole school year. But she agreed to go back to Grandmother Wilkey's for the ninth grade. She went to a high school in El Paso where there were both boys and girls.

At the beginning of school, Cita couldn't believe how Sandra had changed during her year on the ranch. She came to Austin High, "tall and tan and so pretty in her white dress," her friend said. She seemed somewhat shy, but she made many friends and continued to work hard in high school. In June, 1946, when she was only sixteen, she graduated near the top of her class.

From the time she was tiny, Sandra had listened to Grandmother Wilkey telling her "she could do anything she wanted to do." Her parents were also telling her the same thing. No wonder Sandra knew exactly what she wanted to do next.

3

Down on the "Farm"

Sandra had grown up hearing Harry speak about the Stanford University campus. He told her how the red-tiled roofs and pale pink sandstone walls sparkled. He talked about the green palms of the main drive and the rolling hills beyond. It might have been an Arizona setting he was describing for her, instead of Palo Alto, California.

Now that Sandra was ready to go to college, Stanford was her first and only choice. She filled out Stanford's admission forms with great care, answering every question fully. When she came to one that asked her to describe her future goals, she explained that she wanted to get an education and then return to Arizona to be a cattle woman.

It didn't even occur to Sandra that she would not be accepted at Stanford and that she should apply elsewhere just in case. Luckily, with her excellent grades and broad interests, Sandra was exactly the type of student Stanford wanted. She was quickly accepted, and the whole family celebrated.

Over the summer, Sandra prepared the clothing she would take. She and her mother made a trip into Phoenix to buy her some new dresses and shoes. Arriving at Stanford that fall, she found the campus as beautiful as Harry had described it. It was a sprawling, almost rural setting. No wonder it had been nicknamed "The Farm."

It did not take Sandra long to become friendly with Diane and Maribeth. Their rooms were around the corner from hers. Diane also had grown up on a ranch, in a small Southern California community. Maribeth came from Chico, a tiny Northern California city. With their similar backgrounds, they called themselves the "small-town girls" and formed what would become lifelong friendships.

Outwardly, Sandra may have appeared gawky and shy. At sixteen, she was younger than most of the other students. Her clothing was certainly different from the casual outfits of most of the others. They were at home in skirts and sweaters, saddle shoes or penny loafers and bobby socks, while she wore dresses and pumps. But underneath, Sandra brought with her a "self-sufficiency and independence" she had gained from her life on the ranch. She still talked about the Lazy B all the time and planned to take her new friends home to meet M. O. and D. A. (For a long time, she had called her parents by these nicknames, saying each letter of the alphabet as though it were a brand.)

As a freshman, Sandra enrolled in Western Civilization, English, and Spanish, courses she enjoyed and was able to master. Biology was another story. She and Maribeth found it difficult to learn the many parts of the plants and animals they were studying. It was even worse to cut them up. They decided to hire a tutor to help them get through the course. It did raise their grades and Sandra finished with all A's.

Sandra also found time to have fun going to parties and dating young men. One was a handsome fellow who drove a red convertible. When she was being especially silly after a date, she'd waltz along the dormitory halls singing, "Beautiful, beautiful brown eyes," in her lilting Texas drawl.

Sandra hoped to learn about business and government by studying economics. She also hoped to learn how to run a cattle ranch so that it would be successful and make money. She still expected to help run the Lazy B or to find a ranch of her own.

One Sunday evening, Maribeth took Sandra to her uncle's home. Professor Rathbun held weekly get-togethers to introduce students to his ideas about life and ethics. He was a professor in the law school. He expected a great deal from his students, not just in classes, but in the way they lived their lives.

Sandra was spellbound by Professor Rathbun's ideas and his belief that each person could make a difference. She realized the field of law would allow her to help people "on a very personal level." The Lazy B might have to wait a little longer while she went on to law school.

A new rule allowed students to apply to law school after only three years of college. The rule had been established in 1945, after the Second World War ended, to allow returning servicemen to finish school sooner. But it didn't keep women from applying to law school. Stanford had been accepting women since the 1920s, although many Eastern schools did not accept them even 30 years later.

During the first year, Sandra took courses in contracts, as well as civil and criminal law. Looking back, she remembered how she "thoroughly enjoyed law school. . . . I loved my classes."

After classes, she and a new friend, Beatrice, often

sat on the steps to talk over ideas they had just heard. Sometimes they went to the law library to read about the cases they would study the next day.

But they did not spend every moment studying, even in law school. They both lived in Cubberley House, a beautiful old home that was now a cooperative living center for women students. Every few weeks, Sandra and Beatrice might be partners to prepare dinner for the other 30 women who were their housemates. Sometimes they whipped up a casserole of Spanish rice to accompany pork chops. Another time they prepared several meat loaves. Sandra enjoyed cooking and Beatrice thought she was a "wonderful, natural cook."

Sandra's grades continued to be excellent. In her second year, she was selected to be an editor of the *Stanford Law Review*. This honor was given only to students at the top of their class.

While she was writing an article for the *Review*, she met sandy-haired John O'Connor, who was a year behind her in school. They had been asked to work on the same article and were each checking law cases in the library. John suggested they continue working in a nearby restaurant. They spread their papers out on the table and finished the article. Then they began to talk and get to know each other.

Sandra found John's quick sense of humor and wit

very appealing. He loved being able to make her laugh. They spent almost every evening together, studying and then talking about what was important to them. It didn't take very long for them to decide to marry.

Sandra graduated third in her law school class in 1952, when she was 22. Naturally she expected to find a position in a good legal office. She sent out letters to law firms listed on the bulletin board, only to discover those firms were not hiring women lawyers. It didn't matter how well she had done in law school.

It was the same answer every time she applied. Finally, one law office seemed interested. Sandra was excited, until she realized they wanted her to become a secretary for the firm, not a lawyer.

Sandra was tough. She had dealt with too little rain and powerful storms on the ranch. She was not going to let a lack of jobs get her down. She decided to find a place where "people *were* hiring women."

San Mateo County was searching for an attorney to serve on the county's staff. She was offered the job in Redwood City. This was close to Stanford and to John, who was completing his last year of law school.

Sandra liked the people she worked with and learned a great deal as she handled cases for the

county. She found she was given more responsibility, more quickly, than she would have had in a private law firm. And she found herself "right in the middle of public service"—a place she liked to be.

4

Love and Law

John and Sandra planned to marry in the living room of the Lazy B in December, 1952. They went up to the mountains to cut Christmas trees and brought back as much greenery as they could carry. They decorated every inch of the barn with deep green trees and branches. For the party after their marriage ceremony, they had turned Harry's new barn into a magical, fragrant forest.

Their guests came from miles around to dance to the music of a local cowboy band. They feasted on

Lazy B beef that had been roasted in a pit barbecue. The newlyweds had a joyous time at their own wedding, dancing and being with family and friends.

Shortly after they were married, John was drafted into the army and sent to Frankfurt, West Germany. He became a lawyer for the United States Army. Sandra was allowed to join him in Frankfurt. She found a job as a civilian—or non-army—lawyer writing legal contracts and helping distribute surplus goods from the Second World War.

Sandra started taking classes in German and found it a beautiful language to speak. She also began to make friends.

She met Helen Blankenburg, a woman who was her mother's age, and the two of them became very close. The Blankenburgs' 16-year-old son was killed during the war. Mrs. Blankenburg could have spent the rest of her life filled with anger over her loss. Instead, she devoted herself to helping others.

Sandra saw her as "a one-person social service agency," and went along with her on calls to the families she helped. Mrs. Blankenburg was a model for Sandra and an example of the kind of person Professor Rathbun had described to his classes.

Germany had been defeated in World War II, almost eight years earlier. There were still reminders of the war in the rubble of bombed-out buildings and shortages in food and clothing. Also, the rest of the world would not let Germany forget how its Nazi soldiers had killed and imprisoned millions of innocent people.

The O'Connors lived in Germany for three years. They saw the German people trying to rebuild their lives and their country.

When Sandra and John returned to the United States, they had to decide where to live. They chose Phoenix, Arizona. Sandra's college friend Diane was pleased because she and her husband already lived in Phoenix. She also knew the O'Connors would work hard and make a difference to their community.

In order to practice law in Phoenix, the O'Connors needed to pass the Arizona bar exam, a test of the state's laws. They studied for weeks and took the exam together. Both of them passed. Then John quickly found a job in a law firm, but Sandra again discovered that positions for women were not available.

She decided to open an office with a young man who had studied for the Arizona bar exam with the O'Connors. As a private attorney, she was called upon to handle many different kinds of cases. She wrote wills, landlords' leases, and business contracts. She defended people who had been accused of drunk driving or theft.

Sandra felt the most important work she did in

those years was to defend clients too poor to select a lawyer. "I don't think any legal service for which I was paid gave me as much satisfaction as helping someone who needed it," she said later.

Their first son, Scott, was born shortly after Sandra took the bar exam in 1958. She found a very capable woman to take care of the baby so that she could continue to work in her law practice. After two years, Brian was born, and then a third son, Jay, was born in 1962. Sandra found it became more difficult to juggle the babies and her work. She decided to take the next years to be at home with the boys.

The O'Connors were living in their own home in Phoenix. They had even shaped many of its adobe bricks themselves as the house was being built. Whenever Sandra could, she took volunteer jobs relating to children and the law. She organized a service to help people without much money get legal advice. She wrote questions for the Arizona state bar exam. She worked for the Republican party, helping local candidates run for office and getting people out to vote.

Sandra's volunteer work required her to be very organized when she was at home, and very organized on every project. She continued to volunteer for five years. Later, she jokingly told an interviewer, "I decided I should go back to paid employment to get a little peace and quiet in my life and I went out and looked for a job." She found that it was still very difficult for a woman to get a job as a lawyer.

She applied for a job with the attorney general's office. Nothing happened. She kept applying and being ignored. But she was not going to give up.

At last, in 1965, she was hired as an assistant attorney general for the state of Arizona. Her employers sent her to solve the problems of the Arizona State Hospital for the Mentally Ill.

She set up an office in the hospital and began talking to the hospital staff. She learned that there were not good state laws for admitting patients to the hospital to get treatment. Nor were there good laws for sending patients home after treatment. Once she knew what the problems were, she was able to help find solutions.

Sandra worked for other departments in state government. She worked for the welfare department, and the treasurer's office, becoming familiar with the problems they faced. Because each new setting was different, she had to start at the beginning. At the same time, she was building a strong understanding of how state government works.

Recently, she talked about those years with Bill Moyers in a television interview. She told him, "It isn't easy to have both a career and a family." And while she admitted it left her with no free time, she would not have changed a thing: "I've loved my family dearly and I wouldn't have given that up for anything."

5

Tactful But Tough

When Sandra heard there was an empty seat in the Arizona state senate, she decided she wanted to become a state senator. That would allow her to change bad laws and write new laws.

She also thought it would give her a chance to do valuable work, but on a part-time basis. In those years, legislators did not have full-time positions. She would still have time for her family when they needed her.

The County Board of Supervisors appointed her. Sandra campaigned and won the position two more times. In all, she served five years in the Arizona state senate.

In 1972, the Republican senators elected Sandra to become their leader. Because there were more Republicans in the senate, they were called the majority. She was the first woman in the whole country to serve as a majority leader. The senators liked the way she listened to their different ideas and then put all the ideas together. They felt she always did her homework and knew everything there was to know about the subject they were discussing.

Sandra was not afraid to speak out for what she believed important. One news magazine described her as tactful, but tough.

She was also very careful in writing laws, trying to make the wording clear and the punctuation correct. She wanted to do things right the first time so that they would not have to be redone.

Many of the new laws she helped write would benefit women, children, and the poor. She also got rid of bad laws, such as the law that limited a woman, but not a man, to an 8-hour workday, and the law that said a woman's property was controlled by her husband. She changed laws for the mentally ill because she had seen what was needed when she worked at the state hospital.

Sandra kept saying she didn't feel unusual to be the

first woman majority leader. There were several other women in the senate with her. There had been four other women in her law school graduating class. It was more important to her that she was doing good work in every position she held. Even when she was a child working on the Lazy B, no one had made a big deal about her being a girl. They had expected her to do her job.

In all her later jobs, whether volunteer or paid, she admitted, "I worked as hard as I could. I became indispensable and then asked for less time." She made herself so necessary to the job that her employer could not do without her. Then when she worked longer hours than she was paid for, the employer allowed her to take time off to attend her sons' school programs.

The O'Connor boys were growing up and Sandra felt it was important for each of them to find his own special interest and develop skills in something he enjoyed. She signed them up for all kinds of after-school activities. She hired a young man from the nearby high school to be a companion when she or John could not.

When he was older, Brian said, "You name it, we were signed up: Spanish, golf, football, and dancing lessons. If my mother is not busy organizing something or giving directions, she's not happy." Scott became a champion swimmer, Brian a businessman at eight, as he tended the neighbors' yards. Jay played in the school band and then became a star in school plays.

Halloween was a special holiday for the family. They worked together to make their home into a haunted house. Sandra peeled bunches of grapes, turning them into a bowl full of slimy eyeballs. Then she dressed up as a wicked witch who told scary stories. John became a monster who scared the trick-or-treaters with his spooky noises. He also arranged a background of eerie music to complete the scene.

The boys spent most of their summers on the Lazy B. Sandra's brother, Alan, was in charge of running the ranch after Harry retired in 1964. He expected his nephews to work hard, and to dress properly. At a time when they might have wanted to let their hair grow long or use bad language, Uncle Alan saw to it that they followed his strict rules.

When the boys were at home, Sandra and John divided up the parenting responsibilities. She took the emergency calls during the day. John shared other calls with her. They took turns attending school programs. She drove early morning car pool. As soon as Scott was sixteen, he was able to drive his brothers wherever they needed to go.

The three O'Connor boys became very indepen-

dent and resourceful. Once, their dog was run over by a car. The boys removed a door from its hinges to use as a stretcher and carried the injured animal to the vet's office. Another time, they found a swarm of bees in a wall of the house. They called around until they found a beekeeper who would come to get rid of the hive.

By 1974, Sandra had served five years in the Arizona state senate. Now she felt she would like to move from the legislature to the courtroom.

She ran for trial judge in the Superior Court of Maricopa County. The election forced her to get out and fight for the job she wanted.

When she won, she was sworn in as Judge O'Connor. She took her seat in the courtroom, on the "judge's bench." What may have been a bench long ago is now just a high-backed chair. She wore the special black robe worn by judges as a symbol of their long years of study. But she also found another use for her robe when Halloween came around. It was perfect to wear when she greeted the neighborhood children as the Wicked Witch.

In the courtroom, she had serious duties. She had to know state and federal laws. She had to advise attorneys when they were not serving their clients' needs. She had to make sure each attorney followed court rules while defending a client. She had to tell the jury how to use the information they were being given about a case.

When a jury found a person guilty of a crime, she had to sentence that person to serve time in jail or to pay a fine. Once she had to pass sentence on a mother with two small children. She had sentenced the woman to serve a prison term for cashing thousands of dollars' worth of bad checks. She could not overlook the woman's crimes, no matter how badly she felt about the small children. But she went into her office chambers and cried.

Even worse was having to sentence a convicted criminal to death when it was necessary. She never got over the pain that caused her.

In 1979, Governor Babbitt appointed Sandra to the Arizona Court of Appeals. He thought she was "the finest talent available. . . . Her intellectual ability and her judgment are astonishing," he told the press.

The Constitution of the United States set up the court system of our country. There are state and local courts and there are federal courts. Sandra first served as a judge in the county court system and was now moving to the state appeals court. The appeals court deals with cases that have been heard before.

If either person in a case did not like a verdict, or decision, they could ask for the case to be heard again in the appeals court. As an appeals court judge, Sandra would make the decision without a jury. Juries do not hear appeals.

Judge O'Connor reviewed the transcript, or record, from the trial of the case. She might find mistakes in the way the attorneys instructed their jury. She might find disagreements between what witnesses said on the stand. Her decision might be the same or different from the judgment in the lower court.

As an appellate court judge, it became her duty to look at the law and to question the way it had been used by the trial court judge. Lawyers who appeared in her courtroom said that she was a fair, but strict judge. She might not smile much, but she knew the law.

Sandra admits that each time she took a new job, she did not feel sure of herself at first. "I used to be very nervous about public appearances. . . . I would be shaking, even my head. I was terrified even when I got married, the first time in court as a lawyer, the first time I sat on the bench as a trial judge," she said.

"One of the wonderful things about growing older is that you get over your terror. It is a fabulous blessing of advancing age. The more you do something, the easier it gets, and I now am no longer nervous in making public speeches or appearances," she said, with a big grin. "I've done enough of it."

6

Supreme Court Justice

In June, 1981, President Ronald Reagan decided to keep a campaign promise he had made. He would add a woman to the Supreme Court to replace Justice Potter Stewart, who was retiring. He asked his advisers to bring him a list of qualified women.

Sandra Day O'Connor was a strong favorite on the list because she had experience in all three branches of the government.

To let people get to know her, Sandra began a round of meetings. She met with the Attorney General of the United States. She met with other federal attorneys. She met with President Reagan. She talked to senators and congressmen in Washington. Everyone was impressed with her.

Sandra returned to Phoenix asking herself if she was ready to make such a big change in her life. She worried about putting her family in the spotlight. She also felt sad about giving up their home and friends in Phoenix, and leaving the desert surroundings they loved.

John and the boys wanted her to try for the job. And deep down, she must have known she could not pass up this historic chance to serve her country and to become the first woman on the Supreme Court.

She knew that by 1981, there had been 101 justices, all male. Women had not even been allowed to vote until 1920. They could not serve on juries in all fifty states for another 50 years. They did not become judges in every state until 1979.

The first step in being approved was to meet with the Senate Judiciary Committee. Sandra came back to Washington to practice questions and answers with justice department attorneys. She told them it reminded her of the days when she had studied for her bar exam many years before. Now she needed to learn as much as possible about past Supreme Court decisions and to understand how they would influence future cases.

One observer wrote that the opening day of hearings resembled "a wedding." Chairman Strom Thurmond escorted Sandra into the room on his arm. Committee members rushed to shake hands with her. The senators welcomed her warmly in their opening remarks.

Sandra sat facing the senators and "did not seem nervous at all, but her husband did," said a reporter. She introduced John and their sons and told the Committee that this experience had made them all feel even closer than they normally were.

For three days, the Committee questioned her about every aspect of her past and tried to discover how she would vote on future issues that might come before the Supreme Court. She explained that she could not tell them. That would force her to "prejudge" cases before she knew all the facts. The vote taken, on September 15, was 17–0 in favor of passing her name on to the full Senate.

The next week, she appeared before the Senate. Most of the discussion centered on praising the president for selecting O'Connor and praising her for her accomplishments. On September 21, 1981, the Senate voted 99–0, with one senator absent, to confirm Sandra Day O'Connor as the 102nd justice to the Supreme Court.

She was very moved by their support, telling the

senators, "I am absolutely overjoyed." She hoped they would still support her after she had been on the job for ten years.

The swearing-in ceremony was held in the Courtroom of the Supreme Court on Friday, September 25. Looking radiant, Sandra took her oath before her parents, John, their sons, and several hundred friends. President Reagan, smiling broadly, was also there.

She swore to be a fair judge, ". . . and do equal right to the poor and to the rich." The Court's marshal assisted her in putting on her black robe, the same robe she had worn as an Arizona judge. Then the Court's marshal led her to the front of the Court where the other eight justices sat.

Seats on the Supreme Court have a long tradition. The chief justice always sits in the middle. Sandra, as the newest, or junior justice, was seated to the far right. A few years later, when a new justice joined the Court after her, she moved to the seat on the far left. With the next new justice, she moved again, to the second seat from the right.

Justice O'Connor spent her first few days on the job learning her way around the Supreme Court building. She kept getting lost in the broad marble hallways where all the tall doorways looked the same. Often she turned one direction when her chambers were really the opposite way.

Her two-room chambers soon reflected her Arizona roots. She hung paintings of Southwestern landscapes and placed Indian rugs, baskets, and clay pots everywhere.

Sandra had always believed exercise for her body was as important as exercise for her mind. For years, she played a good game of tennis. Then she decided to learn golf and worked hard to become a good golfer. She likes to play well and to win. In the winter she skis, in the summer she goes rafting and hiking, often with her friends, Diane and Maribeth.

She knew she would be putting in long hours reading law cases at the Court each day, and she decided it made sense to start an exercise program right there. She invited the women law clerks and employees to join her first thing in the morning.

They arrive dressed in leotards and special T-shirts reading *Loosen Up with the Supremes*. After a hard physical workout, they shower and change into business clothes, and are ready to get to work on Court business.

To help with their work, each justice hires law school graduates to serve as law clerks for a year. Justice O'Connor usually has four clerks who study cases in the Court library and discuss all sides of a case with her, often while they munch on popcorn. If they have free time, she takes her clerks with her to a baseball game or a museum, as a break from the tiring schedule they all keep.

The Supreme Court receives requests to hear almost 5,000 cases each year. If at least four justices wish to accept a case, it will be heard in the next term. About 150 cases are heard between October and June. The Court takes cases presenting issues of federal law that lower courts do not agree upon and that are important to many people in the country. As Justice O'Connor says, the cases we hear are "very difficult cases."

A case accepted for hearing will be decided within the following six to twelve months. Lawyers for both sides send written notes, or briefs, for the justices to study. They will also be given 30 minutes to speak to the justices during oral argument. In that time, the lawyers are expected to tell the most important points of the case. The justices may ask questions about what is being said or about the written briefs.

After oral arguments, the justices meet alone, without their clerks, to discuss and to vote on their decision in the case. Five of the nine justices must be in agreement for the case to be decided by a majority. The chief justice asks one of them to write the majority opinion. The others may decide to write separate opinions which explain their own thinking. The decisions will be announced to the public when they are completed, several months later.

Justice O'Connor has written some strong opinions. In one case, the Women's University of Mississippi was trying to prevent a male nursing student from entering the school. She wrote that it was unconstitutional for a state-sponsored nursing school to keep male students out. In her opinion, the Fourteenth Amendment to the Constitution was being violated.

The Amendment granted equal rights to all citizens. A well-qualified male student should be allowed to study at the nursing school.

Justice O'Connor warned the other justices that it was important for all of them not to make "inaccurate assumptions about the proper roles of men and women." Just because nurses usually have been women, it doesn't mean men can't be excellent nurses.

In 1989, she ruled in a case about the burning of the American flag. Five justices felt that the First Amendment right of free speech also protects burning the flag as a form of protest. Theirs became the majority opinion. They explained that a young Texas man was expressing that right when he burned the flag. Four justices disagreed, including Justice O'Connor. They wrote a separate opinion, explaining their ideas and how they used the laws to help them reach a decision.

In another case, Justice O'Connor agreed that a Christmas tree and a Hanukkah menorah could be displayed together near the city hall because the government was not choosing Judaism over Christianity. Earlier, she had voted that a nativity scene placed inside the county courthouse was unconstitutional because, standing alone, it seemed to give approval to Christianity.

Her opinions are not always popular. In the 1990s,

one of the most difficult questions facing the Court will be whether a woman has the right to choose to give birth to a child. To what extent does the federal Constitution protect a woman's decision to have an abortion? Pro-choice groups insist that state governments should not be able to force a woman to have a child if she chooses to have an abortion. Pro-life groups do not want the woman to have that choice. They want the Court to uphold laws that prevent, or at least limit, abortions.

Both groups are trying to influence Justice O'Connor because she is the only woman on the Court. Many people write angry letters telling her how to vote. Many march in front of the Supreme Court or interrupt her when she gives speeches around the country. Just as she does with other cases, Justice O'Connor must study the Constitution and all the previous decisions made by the courts before she can make a decision.

She explains that, over time, the Court changes its mind on issues. "There is never an absolute end to any issue . . . there is a continuing dialogue between the Court, the Congress, and the nation as a whole."

As busy as she is with Court matters, she still manages to keep in touch with people and places from her past. Returning to Radford School several years ago, she stood before the students—now boys as well

as girls. No longer trembling as she had in earlier years, she reminded the children to do their best at whatever job they were given, because then they would be ready for any opportunity to come in the future.

She continues to reach out to young people as she did when she invited a visiting student from Kenya, Africa, to have Thanksgiving dinner with her family in Washington. Sandra had been in Kenya in 1982, where women were thrilled to meet her and where she learned about their goals to become future leaders of their country and to improve education and living conditions for their people. Justice O'Connor was a symbol for them, just as she is for many women in the United States.

Outsiders call her distant, reserved, even "schoolmarmish." But friends talk about her loyalty and warmth. Reporters often ask her husband, John, how he feels about having such an important wife. "Sandra's accomplishments don't make me a lesser man; they make me a fuller man," he once answered. Because Sandra's work is so serious, she finds John's "sense of humor a tonic," saying he has kept her "laughing for more than thirty years."

One of Sandra's personal dreams was to have grandchildren. Her wish came true in the fall of 1989, when her oldest son's wife gave birth to a daughter, just in time for Halloween. To celebrate, her law clerks created a "Grandma Justice"—a pumpkin head dressed in judge's robes, with a baby pumpkin doll on its lap.

Sandra admits that the "Founding Fathers" of our Constitution would be pretty surprised to know a woman is on the Supreme Court interpreting the Constitution. She thought even Thomas Jefferson might have had difficulty with the idea. He "indicated on a number of occasions that he didn't think the nation was ready to see a woman in public office, nor was he."

Since the Constitution was written, wise women and men haved waged battles to win rights for women. Justice O'Connor never forgets all those who paved the way for her to become the first woman on the Supreme Court.

She also remembers and repeats what her Stanford professor taught her years earlier. "The individual can make things happen," she told students in a graduation speech. She will continue to use her position on the Supreme Court to do just that.

ABOUT THIS BOOK

I went to Washington, D.C., to meet with Justice Sandra Day O'Connor. I wanted to learn how she had been able to accomplish so much at a time when most women did not have the opportunity. "I just assumed that I could do what I wanted," she explained. She never thought of herself as special.

I kept searching for clues. One friend described her unique ability to concentrate: "When she's working, she's working. When she's playing tennis, she's playing tennis. When she's at a party, she's at a party." And her brother adds that she does every job "to perfection . . . better than anyone else."

There is no question that her standards for herself are high. She is also a wonderful role model for others. A young college woman led me on a tour of the Supreme Court, and confided that she had been a sophomore in high school when Justice O'Connor took her seat on the Court. It gave her a message that she could do anything in the world she wanted to do—the same message Grandmother Wilkey had given young Sandra Day from the beginning.

—B. G.